Dear Parents:

Congratulations! Your child is taking the first steps on an exciting journey. The destination? Independent reading!

STEP INTO READING® will help your child get there. The program offers five steps to reading success. Each step includes fun stories and colorful art or photographs. In addition to original fiction and books with favorite characters, there are Step into Reading Non-Fiction Readers, Phonics Readers and Boxed Sets, Sticker Readers, and Comic Readers—a complete literacy program with something to interest every child.

Learning to Read, Step by Step!

Ready to Read   Preschool–Kindergarten
• big type and easy words • rhyme and rhythm • picture clues
For children who know the alphabet and are eager to begin reading.

Reading with Help   Preschool–Grade 1
• basic vocabulary • short sentences • simple stories
For children who recognize familiar words and sound out new words with help.

Reading on Your Own   Grades 1–3
• engaging characters • easy-to-follow plots • popular topics
For children who are ready to read on their own.

Reading Paragraphs   Grades 2–3
• challenging vocabulary • short paragraphs • exciting stories
For newly independent readers who read simple sentences with confidence.

Ready for Chapters   Grades 2–4
• chapters • longer paragraphs • full-color art
For children who want to take the plunge into chapter books but still like colorful pictures.

STEP INTO READING® is designed to give every child a successful reading experience. The grade levels are only guides; children will progress through the steps at their own speed, developing confidence in their reading. The F&P Text Level on the back cover serves as another tool to help you choose the right book for your child.

Remember, a lifetime love of reading starts with a single step!

For kids who love hot dogs
—J.M.

Text copyright © 2015 by Julianne Moore
Cover art and interior illustrations copyright © 2015 by LeUyen Pham

All rights reserved. Published in the United States by Random House Children's Books, a division of Random House LLC, a Penguin Random House Company, New York.

Step into Reading, Random House, and the Random House colophon are registered trademarks of Random House LLC.

Visit us on the Web!
StepIntoReading.com
randomhousekids.com

Educators and librarians, for a variety of teaching tools, visit us at RHTeachersLibrarians.com

Library of Congress Cataloging-in-Publication Data
Moore, Julianne.
Freckleface Strawberry : lunch, or what's that? / Julianne Moore ; illustrated by LeUyen Pham.
pages cm. — (Step into reading. Step 2)
Summary: "Freckleface Strawberry and Windy Pants Patrick are wary of the school lunch."
—Provided by publisher.
ISBN 978-0-385-39192-4 (trade) — ISBN 978-0-375-97366-6 (lib. bdg.) —
ISBN 978-0-385-39191-7 (pbk.) — ISBN 978-0-385-39193-1 (ebook)
[1. Best friends—Fiction. 2. Friendship—Fiction. 3. Luncheons—Fiction. 4. School lunchrooms, cafeterias, etc.—Fiction.] I. Pham, LeUyen, illustrator. II. Title. III. Title: Lunch, or what's that?
PZ7.M78635Frp 2015
[E]—dc23
2014040653

Printed in the United States of America

10 9 8 7 6 5 4 3 2 1

This book has been officially leveled by using the F&P Text Level Gradient™ Leveling System.

FRECKLEFACE STR🍓WBERRY
Lunch, or WHAT'S THAT?

by Julianne Moore
illustrated by LeUyen Pham

Random House 🏠 New York

Chapter 1

Freckleface Strawberry
and Windy Pants Patrick
both loved to eat lunch.

They loved
to eat
hot dogs.

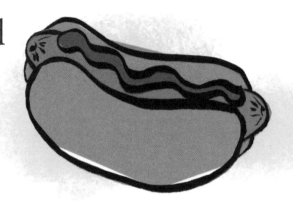

They loved
to eat
grilled cheese.

They loved to eat
peanut butter and jelly.

They loved to eat
chicken fingers.

They loved
to eat noodles.

They loved to eat.

They loved to eat lunch,
but they did NOT
love to eat lunch
in the lunch room.

Chapter 2

One day,
Freckleface Strawberry
and Windy Pants Patrick
went to the lunch room.

Freckleface Strawberry
got into the lunch line.
She put her lunch
on the tray.

She sat down next to
Windy Pants.

Freckleface Strawberry
was ready to eat.

"What is that?"
Windy Pants Patrick asked.
"That?" said Freckleface.
"That is lunch."

"I know that is lunch,"
  said Windy Pants.
"But WHAT is it?"
"I do not know,"
  said Freckleface.

Chapter 3

Then Winnie sat down.
"What is that?" said Winnie.
"What?" said Freckleface.
"That," said Winnie.

"That is lunch,"
  said Freckleface.
"Oh," said Winnie.
"But what is it?"
  Freckleface said sadly,
"I do not know."

Then Noah sat down.
"How is lunch?" Noah yelled.
"I do not know,"
said Freckleface.

"Why not?"
asked Noah loudly.
"Because THAT is lunch,"
said Freckleface.
She pointed at her tray.

"That?" cried Noah.
"THAT is lunch?"
"YES!" shouted Freckleface,
Windy Pants, and Winnie.

"Shhhhhhhhhhhhh!"
said the lunch room teacher.
"No yelling in
the lunch room.
Only lunch eating."

"Well, it IS time for
    lunch eating," Freckleface
    Strawberry whispered.
"It is MY lunch.
    I GUESS I will eat it."

Chapter 4

Windy Pants Patrick,
Winnie, and Noah
were very, very quiet.
Freckleface Strawberry
ate her lunch.

Windy Pants, Winnie,
and Noah watched her eat.
Windy Pants, Winnie,
and Noah were
very, very curious.

Freckleface Strawberry
chewed a long time.
Finally, Windy Pants
Patrick said, "What is it?"

Freckleface Strawberry
shook her head.
"I do not know,"
she said. . . .

"But I LIKE it!"

And then they all
ate lunch.